THE GREAT GOLD RUSH ADVENTURE

For Jennie and Walter

Special thanks to Ben Grossblatt.

Library of Congress Cataloging-in-Publication Data is available.
ISBN: 9780986086786

Printed in China
First edition 2016

Miners Landing Press
1301 Alaskan Way
Seattle, WA 98101
Please visit us at www.minerslandingpress.com

Produced by Girl Friday Productions, LLC
www.girlfridayproductions.com

• MINERS LANDING PRESS PRESENTS •

THE GREAT GOLD RUSH ADVENTURE

KYLE GRIFFITH

ILLUSTRATED BY JIM STARR

It all started when the SS *Portland* arrived at Seattle's Pier 57 carrying two tons of gold and tales of fortunes just waiting to be plucked from the ground. Klondike fever was a sickness no doctor could cure, and everyone had it bad. Thousands were willing to risk everything—their savings, their health, even their lives—for a chance to strike it rich in the goldfields of the North. Seattle was a young city then, a small city, and life was hard there. But this was going to change.

5

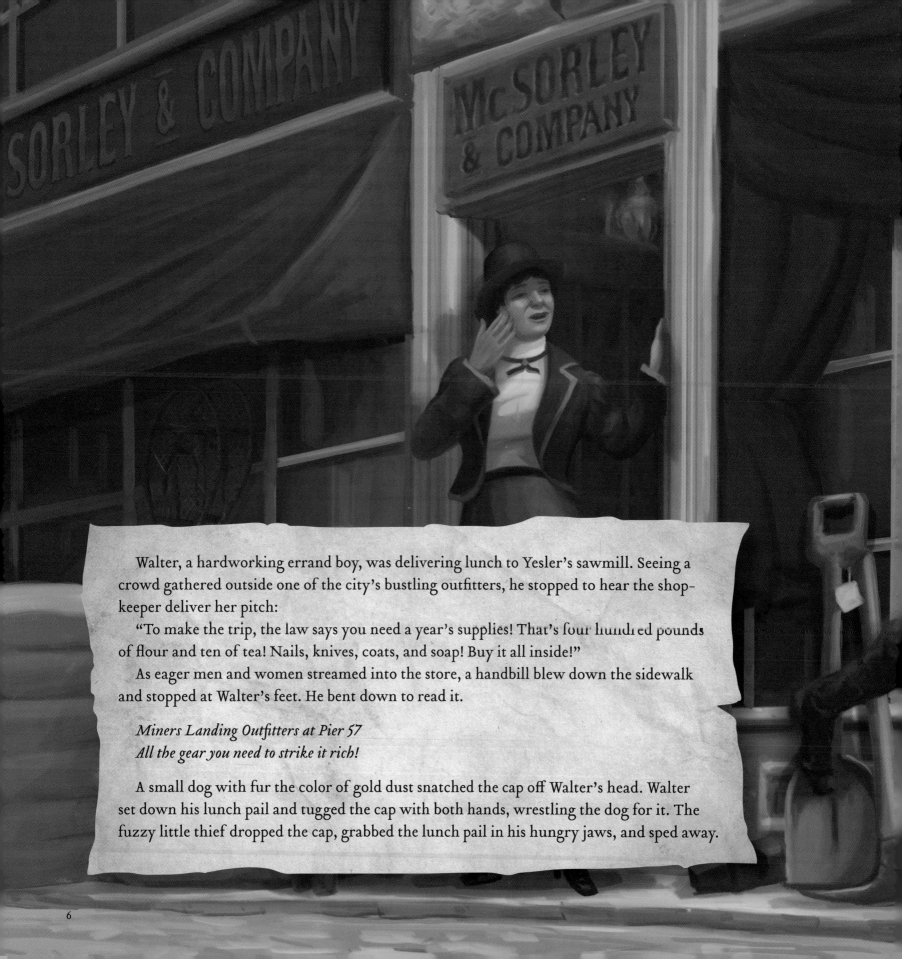

Walter, a hardworking errand boy, was delivering lunch to Yesler's sawmill. Seeing a crowd gathered outside one of the city's bustling outfitters, he stopped to hear the shop-keeper deliver her pitch:

"To make the trip, the law says you need a year's supplies! That's four hundred pounds of flour and ten of tea! Nails, knives, coats, and soap! Buy it all inside!"

As eager men and women streamed into the store, a handbill blew down the sidewalk and stopped at Walter's feet. He bent down to read it.

Miners Landing Outfitters at Pier 57
All the gear you need to strike it rich!

A small dog with fur the color of gold dust snatched the cap off Walter's head. Walter set down his lunch pail and tugged the cap with both hands, wrestling the dog for it. The fuzzy little thief dropped the cap, grabbed the lunch pail in his hungry jaws, and sped away.

Walter chased the dog up First Avenue, through the crowds and past the horses pulling wagons. (The streetcar drivers had all left the city for their chance at Yukon gold.) He splashed down the rutted, swampy street, water seeping through the holes in his shoes. Running as fast as he could, he was just able to keep the little dog in view.

He had to get that lunch pail back. If he didn't make his deliveries for the day, he could kiss those two nickels good-bye.

As they neared Pier 57, where the famous ship *Portland* was just casting off its lines and getting ready to steam out of the bay, the crowds grew even thicker. The little dog leapt between a man's legs and scrambled down the dock, Walter just behind, matching him step for step as they reached the end of the pier!

9

The dog jumped. Walter jumped. A cloud of black smoke puffed from the stack of the *Portland*. Boy and pup landed on the deck amid throngs of passengers.

Everyone with a hope of gold and money enough for a ticket was squeezed onto the deck or into the berths below. The dog scrambled through the passengers and around the crew loading cargo. Finally coming to a stop at the bow of the large ship, the dog flopped onto the deck and started in on the stolen lunch.

A man with a big white bib of a beard looked down on Walter. "And who might you be?" he roared. Then he smiled and held out his hand. "Friend of Dusty's here, are you?" He gave the dog a pat. "Well, any friend of Dusty is a friend of mine! The name's Old Hal, and it looks like you're stuck with us." He couldn't miss the worried look on Walter's face. "Oh, don't be so glum. We'll get word to your folks, and Dusty and I'll look after you."

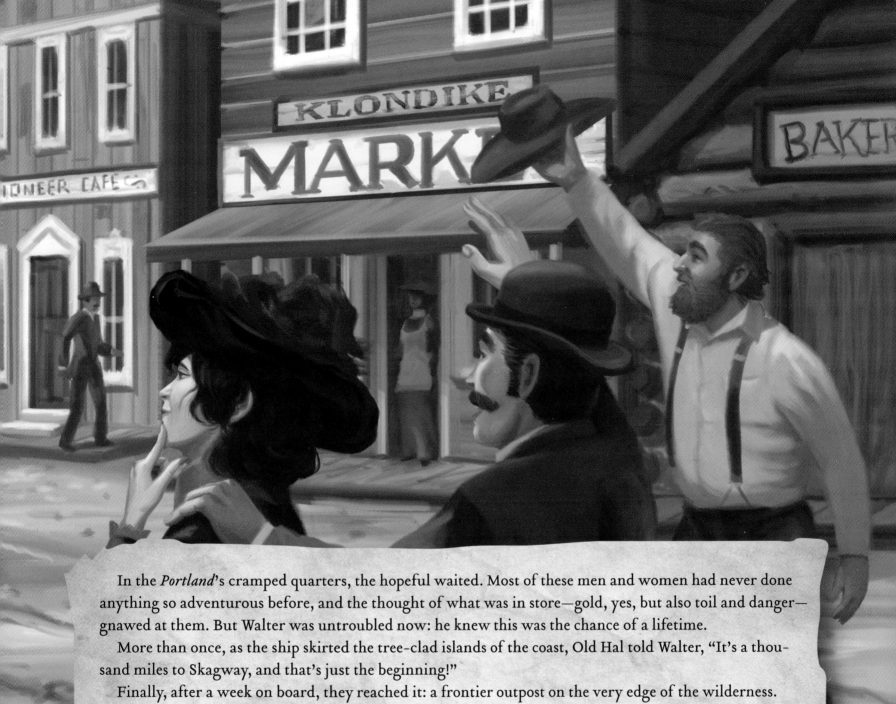

In the *Portland*'s cramped quarters, the hopeful waited. Most of these men and women had never done anything so adventurous before, and the thought of what was in store—gold, yes, but also toil and danger—gnawed at them. But Walter was untroubled now: he knew this was the chance of a lifetime.

More than once, as the ship skirted the tree-clad islands of the coast, Old Hal told Walter, "It's a thousand miles to Skagway, and that's just the beginning!"

Finally, after a week on board, they reached it: a frontier outpost on the very edge of the wilderness. Striding up and down the beach, overseeing the unloading of the *Portland*, was Soapy Smith.

"They call him the king of Skagway," Old Hal said. "I call him a world-class crook. Watch your pockets."

Soapy had a hundred ways to trick would-be miners. While they dreamed of getting rich off gold, Soapy and his gang got rich off *them*.

As Old Hal gathered up their things, Walter stopped a man waiting for a boat back down south. He entrusted him with a letter to his parents in Seattle, so they'd know he was on his way to the goldfields.

WHITE·PASS

CANADIAN·GOLDFIELDS 33 MILES

CHILKOOT TRAIL

YUKON
TTERS

WARE

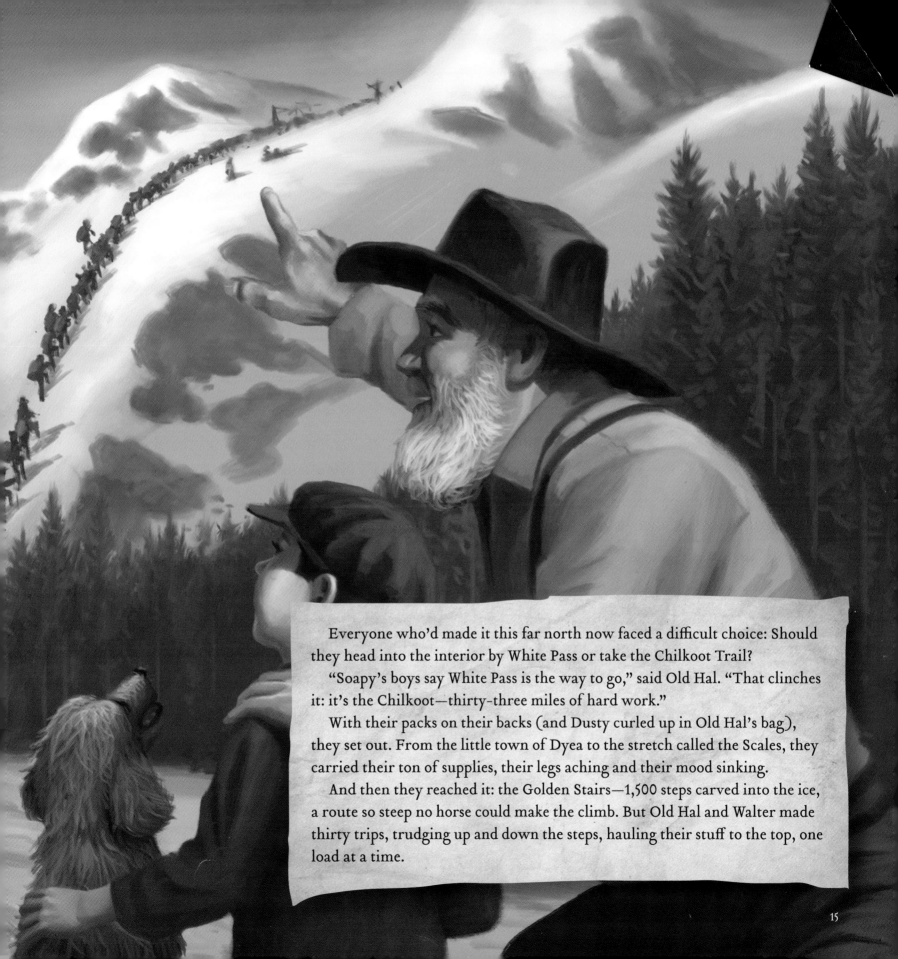

Everyone who'd made it this far north now faced a difficult choice: Should they head into the interior by White Pass or take the Chilkoot Trail?

"Soapy's boys say White Pass is the way to go," said Old Hal. "That clinches it: it's the Chilkoot—thirty-three miles of hard work."

With their packs on their backs (and Dusty curled up in Old Hal's bag), they set out. From the little town of Dyea to the stretch called the Scales, they carried their ton of supplies, their legs aching and their mood sinking.

And then they reached it: the Golden Stairs—1,500 steps carved into the ice, a route so steep no horse could make the climb. But Old Hal and Walter made thirty trips, trudging up and down the steps, hauling their stuff to the top, one load at a time.

"Hey, kid," Old Hal said as they looked down on Lake Bennett and the frozen Yukon River just beyond, the backbreaking Chilkoot Trail finally behind them. "What do you know about building boats?"

Walter knew nothing, Old Hal not much more, but that didn't stop them. Amid thousands of do-it-yourself shipwrights, they cobbled together a makeshift boat just big enough for their crew of three. They stuffed the seams with whatever they could find: unraveled ropes and even a pair of long johns.

At last, when the ice began to break apart in the Yukon River, they set off. After their slog in the mountains, the first fifty miles floating downstream was almost fun. But at White Horse Rapids, the current picked up speed. The river grew so rough Walter was sure they would go under. The rushing, frothing waves snapped at the boat, and from his perch on the bow, Dusty bit back. Old Hal and Walter paddled like crazy.

Where the Yukon met the Klondike River, a boomtown—Dawson City—sprang up like a mushroom after rain. From around the world, gold hunters came by the thousands. Whatever they wanted, Dawson could provide. If you were rich enough, you could eat your supper off plates of gold.

At the Golden Horseshoe Saloon, Old Hal talked with other miners to finalize his plans. While a man played a rickety piano and people danced on tables, Walter saw the same gold watch stolen three times by one pickpocket after another. Dusty got in a little thievery of his own, sneaking stew from an unguarded bowl.

A card game in the corner quickly got out of hand, and angry players started firing pistols and brawling. "Time for us to go, boys!" Old Hal said over the noise, and they tore through the swinging doors into the street.

Back in the saloon Old Hal had paid for a sled and a team of dogs to pull it. Walter thought they looked more like pets—hardly strong enough to pull them and all their supplies—but the dogs soon surprised him. Their fluffy coats flecked with snow, they stood to attention when Old Hal called out, "Mush!" And then they ran, full of the joy of running.

"It won't be long now!" said Old Hal. "We're meeting a fella at the creek, not twenty miles from here! Enjoy the ride!"

And so Walter did. They were speeding so fast, he nearly lost his hat. As the dog team dragged the sled over the slick ground, Dusty was happy to be a passenger, too, and he excitedly watched the wintry scenery from the comfort of Walter's arms.

Twenty miles, Walter thought. *After all this way, we're almost there.*

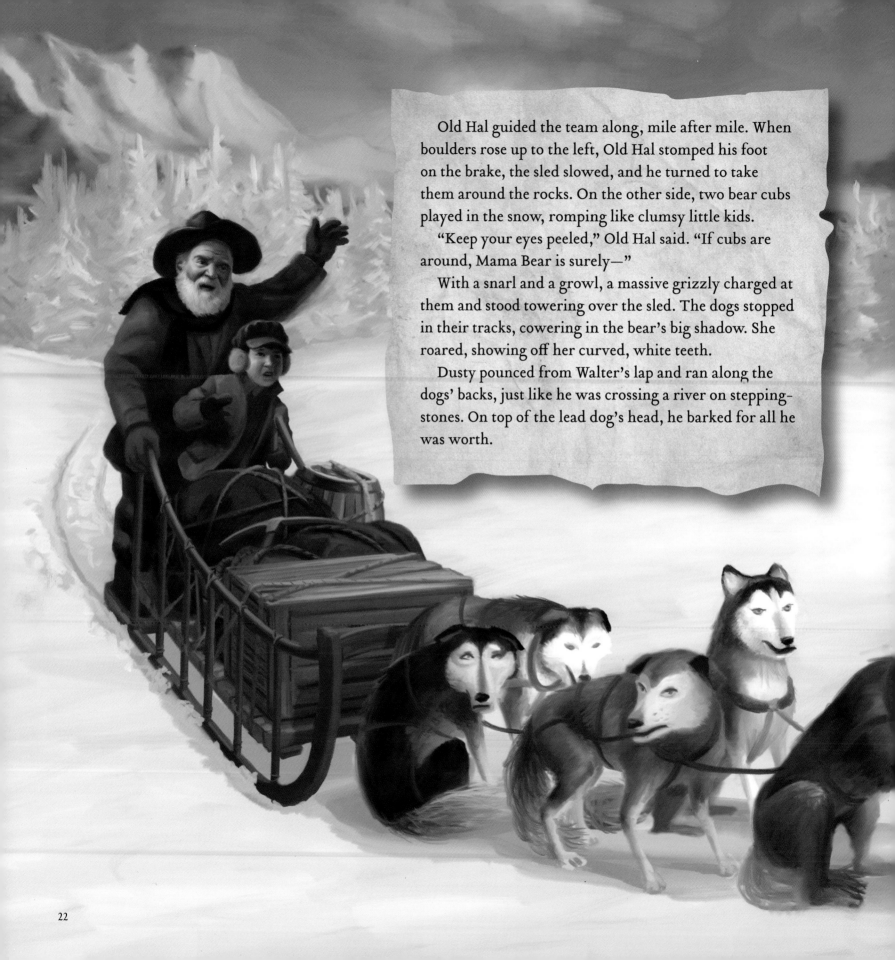

Old Hal guided the team along, mile after mile. When boulders rose up to the left, Old Hal stomped his foot on the brake, the sled slowed, and he turned to take them around the rocks. On the other side, two bear cubs played in the snow, romping like clumsy little kids.

"Keep your eyes peeled," Old Hal said. "If cubs are around, Mama Bear is surely—"

With a snarl and a growl, a massive grizzly charged at them and stood towering over the sled. The dogs stopped in their tracks, cowering in the bear's big shadow. She roared, showing off her curved, white teeth.

Dusty pounced from Walter's lap and ran along the dogs' backs, just like he was crossing a river on stepping-stones. On top of the lead dog's head, he barked for all he was worth.

When it came to sticking up for his friends, Dusty couldn't be beat. The bear gave another growl, but Dusty wasn't backing down. The beast dropped to four feet, the cubs ran to her side, and the whole family trundled away.

Nearby, a head popped up from a large hole in the ground. "Hal!" the shaggy head said. "You made it!"

"Pickax Pete, you flea-bitten old prospector!"

They had finally met up with Old Hal's friend, who had staked this claim half a year before. All around them, men and women were working their patches of ground. Some were shoveling gravel into a rocker box. More were panning for gold in the ice-cold creek, swishing water around in wide metal dishes, hoping to see gleaming specks and flecks. Pete was down in a pit five feet deep with his pickax and his dreams.

"Look for a glimmer in the rock," Pete told Walter. "That's the pay streak, and it means gold."

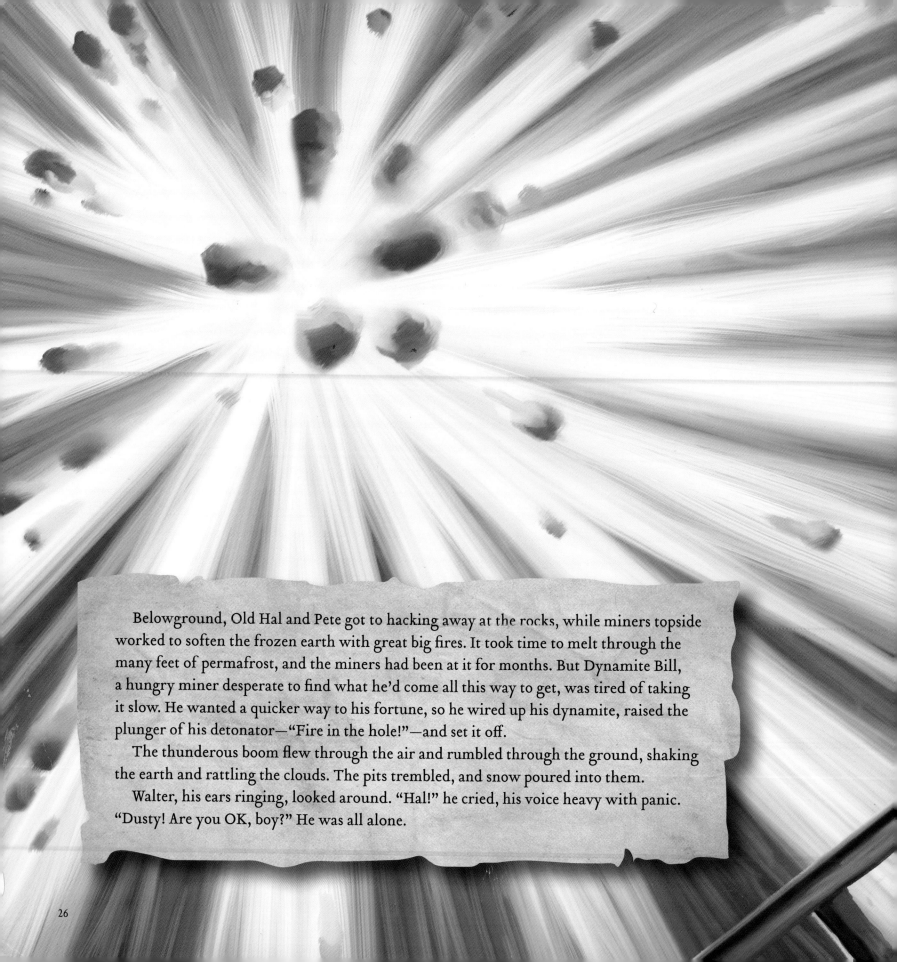

Belowground, Old Hal and Pete got to hacking away at the rocks, while miners topside worked to soften the frozen earth with great big fires. It took time to melt through the many feet of permafrost, and the miners had been at it for months. But Dynamite Bill, a hungry miner desperate to find what he'd come all this way to get, was tired of taking it slow. He wanted a quicker way to his fortune, so he wired up his dynamite, raised the plunger of his detonator—"Fire in the hole!"—and set it off.

The thunderous boom flew through the air and rumbled through the ground, shaking the earth and rattling the clouds. The pits trembled, and snow poured into them.

Walter, his ears ringing, looked around. "Hal!" he cried, his voice heavy with panic. "Dusty! Are you OK, boy?" He was all alone.

The landscape was a white wave in a frozen sea. Everywhere Walter looked, he saw snow and ice, tumbled rocks, and overturned equipment.

Walter heard a familiar, high-pitched bark. Then, wearing a helmet of snow, Dusty ran to his side. He raced around Walter's legs three times, wild with fearful excitement, then ran back the way he had come. Walter followed him on shaky legs until they reached Pete's claim. Dusty jumped into the deep pit and started digging.

His paws scrabbling, his nose sniffing, Dusty worked to free Old Hal, still dazed from the blast and buried up to his chin. Snow went flying as he dug. Soon he had uncovered Old Hal's big beard, frozen stiff as a plank of cedar. He licked Hal's face until he came to.

"Quit it, you mutt! I can take it from here," Old Hal said. "Walter, make sure Pete's all right, too."

It wasn't long before they had dug everyone out of the snow and returned to their search for gold. Not even explosions and avalanches could keep them off the hunt.

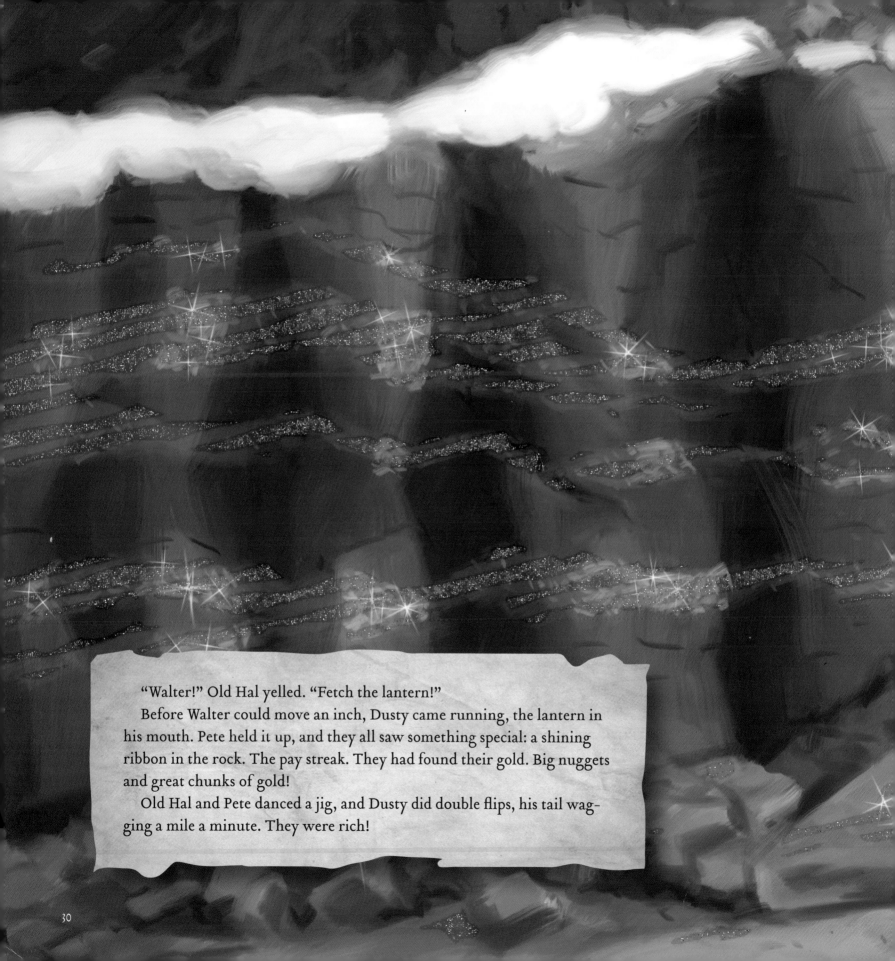

"Walter!" Old Hal yelled. "Fetch the lantern!"

Before Walter could move an inch, Dusty came running, the lantern in his mouth. Pete held it up, and they all saw something special: a shining ribbon in the rock. The pay streak. They had found their gold. Big nuggets and great chunks of gold!

Old Hal and Pete danced a jig, and Dusty did double flips, his tail wagging a mile a minute. They were rich!

All their sweat and tears behind them, they headed south aboard the *Portland*, the same ship that had brought them north. But everything was different. They lived in luxury now. In their cushy stateroom, they were waited on hand and foot   they tipped the steward with a hunk of gold as big as an egg—and they soaked in hot baths for hours, clinking glasses and dining on delicious morsels. When Old Hal said that most of the people who clawed their way to the Klondike in search of gold left empty-handed, bent and broken, Walter bowed his head. Out of a hundred thousand who tried, only a few hundred struck it rich.

A week later, they had made their return to Seattle. Pier 57 was still packed with people welcoming the victorious miners home and seeing off loved ones about to start their own adventures.

At the bottom of the gangplank, Walter and Old Hal shook hands. Walter stooped to give Dusty one last pet, and then he walked off.

"Hey, kid!" Old Hal said. "Don't forget your share."

THE SEATTLE POST-INTELLIGENCER

LATEST NEWS FROM THE KLONDIKE.

GOLD FEVER CONTINUES!

Boy and His Dog Strike it Rich,
Rich, Rich in Alaska.

**Record-Breaking Nugget Rumored
to Weigh Twenty-Two Pounds!**

Additional Prospectors Flock to Find their Fortune

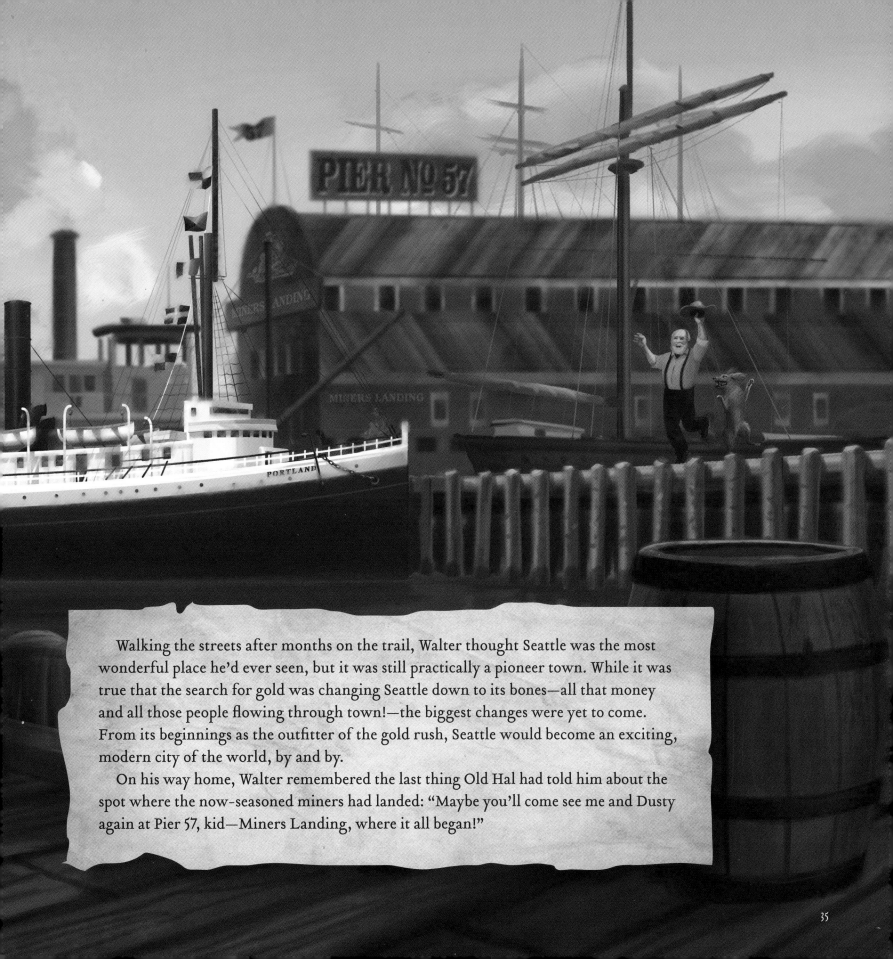

Walking the streets after months on the trail, Walter thought Seattle was the most wonderful place he'd ever seen, but it was still practically a pioneer town. While it was true that the search for gold was changing Seattle down to its bones—all that money and all those people flowing through town!—the biggest changes were yet to come. From its beginnings as the outfitter of the gold rush, Seattle would become an exciting, modern city of the world, by and by.

On his way home, Walter remembered the last thing Old Hal had told him about the spot where the now-seasoned miners had landed: "Maybe you'll come see me and Dusty again at Pier 57, kid—Miners Landing, where it all began!"

MORE ABOUT WALTER'S ADVENTURE

Page 5: You can stand in the same spot where the SS *Portland* docked.
When the SS *Portland* arrived in 1897, Seattle's waterfront looked a lot different than it does today. In fact, today's Piers 57 and 59 (home to the Seattle Aquarium) were bustling docks that received steamships and their goods. The *Portland* actually docked at the now missing Pier 58, then known as Schwabacher Wharf, which was located where Waterfront Park now stands—between Miners Landing and the Seattle Aquarium!

Page 7: That's quite a shopping list!
Back then, some disreputable shopkeepers hoping to sell a bundle of goods told aspiring prospectors that Canadian law required them to have a year's supply of gear. The total weight of one store's recommended clothing, food, and tools: almost 2,400 pounds! In fact, lore has it that some prospectors were convinced to buy diving suits so they could look for gold underwater. Can you find the diving suits in the *Portland*'s cargo hold on page 9?

Filson was one of many fine Seattle retailers that got their start during the gold rush. Another retailer also got its start when John Nordstrom sold his stake in a gold field claim and invested that money to start a shoe store that ultimately became the Nordstrom department store we know today.

Pages 10–11: More about the *Portland*.
The *Portland* was no stranger to riches—or the law. Launched in 1885 and christened the *Haytian Republic*, the ship was built to provide shipping and passenger services from Boston to Haiti. But it was not long before the ship changed hands and was stopped repeatedly for smuggling illegal goods. The ship was refurbished and renamed the SS *Portland*, and shortly after became the famous vessel that brought the first ton of gold to Seattle—officially kicking off the Klondike gold rush. The *Portland* wrecked in 1910, making the rocky shore of Alaska's Katalla Bay its final resting place.

Pictured on pages 10 and 11 is an inside view of how the *Portland* might have looked during the gold rush days. At the top level were the pilot room, bunks for the crew and passengers, and the captain's quarters. The first deck below may have held more sleeping quarters, as well as a dining hall, kitchen, and storage. The lowest level would have been used for storage—all that equipment the passengers brought with them, as well as supplies being delivered to Alaska and even farm animals! The boiler room was—literally—a hot spot on the *Portland*.

Page 14: Those are some smart gophers.
Did people really believe that trained gophers could find gold, or is it a 120-year-old joke? According to an 1897 article in the *Chicago Tribune*, the Consolidated Trans-Alaskan Gopher Company guaranteed a big payout of ten dollars per share—if victims invested one dollar first. That was a lot of money back then, and a lot of bologna!

Page 18: Can you find the mark on the playing card?
Is someone who cheats at cards a "cardsharp" or a "card shark"? Either way you say it, this fishy business